WEST CHICAGO PUBLIC LIBRARY DISTRICT
3 6653 00115 9254
P9-CML-076

BRIAN JACQUES

a Redwall Winter's Tale

illustrated by

CHRISTOPHER DENISE

Philomel Books • New York

For Hannah Elizabeth Jacques with love from Grandad

—B. J.

For my wife, Anika

—C. D.

PATRICIA LEE GAUCH, EDITOR

PHILOMEL BOOKS,
a division of Penguin Putnam Books for Young Readers,
345 Hudson Street, New York, NY 10014.
Philomel Books, Reg. U.S. Pat. & Tm. Off. Published simultaneously in Canada.
Printed in Hong Kong by South China Printing Co. (1988) Ltd.
Designed by Semadar Megged. Text set in Perpetua Bold.

Library of Congress Cataloging-in-Publication Data
Jacques, Brian.
A Redwall winter's tale / by Brian Jacques ; illustrated by Christopher Denise. p. cm.
Summary: Funloving Bungo the molebabe and his friend Tubspike the hedgehog maid
welcome a traveling troupe that visits Redwall Abbey to celebrate the coming
of Snow Badger, the Lord of Wintertide.
[1. Animals—Fiction. 2. Winter—Fiction. 3. Fantasy.] I. Denise, Christopher, ill. II. Title.
PZ7.J15317 Reg 2001 [Fic]—dc21 98-39816

ISBN 0-399-23346-6
1 3 5 7 9 10 8 6 4 2
First Impression

Old leaves were all a-rustling
On Autumn's final day,
North wind was coldly bustling
On Autumn's final day,
Small birds had flown,
Good crops were grown
And harvested away,
On Autumn's final day.

Two little creatures trundled through the leaf-strewn path outside of old Redwall Abbey: Bungo the mole-babe and his friend Tubspike the hedgehog maid. Good Father Abbot had given them permission to welcome some very special guests who were coming to entertain at the Abbey.

Bungo and Tubspike peered anxiously along the path.

"Yurr missy, oi 'opes they'm cumm afore et be dark!" Bungo growled in his funny molevoice.

Tubspike squeaked as the wind tugged at her apron. "If'n you say that once more, I'll roll you in the leaves!"

So he said it once more. The two friends tussled and giggled amid drifts of crispy, crackly, gold and red-brown Autumn leaves.

A flute trilled from the distance
to the beating of a drum:
Tweedly dee, tootley toot! Rubba dub dubba dub dum!
It carried on the blustering breeze
and echoed o'er the leafless trees,
a merry, carefree, happy sound
swirling, twirling, 'round and 'round.
Then came the strains of singing,
of jolly voices ringing
from over the hills and far away
on Autumn's final day!

Wreathed in leaves from tail to snout, Bungo and Tubspike scrambled up, pointing to a gaily colored cart. It was surrounded by a group of creatures, pushing it along the dusty path to Redwall.

Both the little friends shouted excitedly. "They'm yurr! Oi tole ee they'd cumm!" "Sam! Sam! Oh, tell everyone they've arrived!"

Perched on the Abbey's high outer wall, Sam the noisy squirrel bellowed out in his thunderous voice, "Tell the Abbot! They're here, friends. They're here! Sound out the bells!"

This is the song of the bells. Bong boom!
Right joyfully it tells. Bong boom!
'Tis Autumn's final day. Ring a lay!
And so to all we say, ring a lay!
Our doors are open wide. Ding dong!
Come one, come all inside. Ding dong!
Now rest you, traveler, hear our song,
Bong boom ring a lay ding dong!

Every creature in Redwall Abbey came pouring out of the main doors as Sam called and the bells tolled.

Cooks from the kitchens powdered with flour!
Pot washers with paws still dripping!
Candle and lantern lighters, blowing out their tapers!
Firewood gatherers, casting aside their bundles!
Washerbeasts with pegs stuck to ears and tails!
Helpers from the infirmary with bandages streaming out!
Nursery nurses, hugging babes close!
Hedgehogs from the wine cellars in their great aprons!
Table layers, dropping spoons and forks in their haste!

What a crowd ran to the main gates, eager to greet the travelers. Constance the Badgermum brought up the rear, with Foremole and Skipper of otters. Between them they helped the old Father Abbot along.

Wind came whistling out of the north then, bending trees and flattening grass. The creatures around the cart were hooded and cloaked against the cold.

Still covered in leaves, Bungo bowed and Tubspike curtsied to the visitors. They had practiced a long speech of welcome, but the wind bowled them both over. Tubspike took a fit of the chuckles, and Bungo wrinkled his nose at the guests.

"Cumm in, zurrs an' marms, afore ee all freezes!"

Old Father Abbot smiled at Bungo and Tubspike. "Well done, you two! Please, friends, hurry inside. Welcome to Redwall Abbey!"

Outside the skies were bleak
on Autumn's final day.
Last Summer's butterflies
like dreams had passed away.
So come along now, haste, don't bide,
'tis snug and warm and dry inside.
Oh, kindly walk this way,
on Autumn's final day.
Our fields are dark and drear,
the lake lies cold and still,
bold wind from out the north
bends trees unto its will.
Night falls fast now, come, my friend,
goodwill awaits at journey's end.
You've traversed quite a way
on Autumn's final day!

Once they were inside Great Hall, the travelers parked their cart in a corner and set up a gaily hued canvas screen around it. Still wearing hooded cloaks, they disappeared behind the screen.

Matthias the Redwall Warriormouse and his wife, Cornflower, were greatly puzzled until the Abbot explained.

"They will not eat or drink until they have entertained us. Come, my friends, take your places at the table."

Great Hall was lit with candles and colored lanterns. The Winter Feast had been placed on the tables. Happy Redwallers chuckled and gossiped as they sat waiting.

Fat Friar Hugo inspected each dish.

"Hot harvest broth with barley dumplings!

Deep orchard apple pie with blackberries!

Wheat and chestnut bread with celery cheese!

Honeyed pear flan with preserved strawberries!

Leek and mushroom turnover in mint and carrot sauce!

Abbey trifle with meadowcream and candied acorns!"

The list went on and on and on.

Until Bungo and Tubspike interrupted. "Yurr, oi be furr starven, zurr!" "Aye, stop tellin' us about it an' serve it up, Friar!"

Friar Hugo chuckled until his tummy wobbled. "On with the feast, and serve these two rascals first!"

Across the banquet's busy hum
a trumpet brayed to a rolling drum.
As silence fell, a booming call
welled up to the rafters of Great Hall:

" 'Twill soon be Winter's Day,
so the Traveling Thistledown Troupe
will put on a show to astound your eyes
and make you sit up in surprise.
I present our famous group:
the Traveling Thistledown Troupe!"

Amid bangs, pink smoke, and multicolored lights, the canvas screen collapsed. Out sprang the performers, led by a grandly clad hare. He carried a big, curling seashell, which he used to shout into.

"I'm Hypericum Hadduck Hare,
I lead the Thistledown Troupe, y'know.
Whichever way the wind may blow,
that's the jolly old way we'll go!
An' whether the weather is foul or fair,
we'll sing for our supper here an' there.
We're the chaps who'll make you laugh or cry,
bring a smile t'your lips or a tear t'your eye,
and our fee is a trifle, a pudden or soup,
we're the Traveling Thistledown Troupe!"

Three pretty mousemaids burst into song, fluttering their eyelashes at the astonished Redwallers.

"I'm Crotchet! I'm Quaver! I'm Queenie!
The Three Melodious Mice!
We've sung at lots of harvest fayres
And at some banquets twice.
If you love to hear a ballad, dear,
Please take our sound advice:
Don't fret or fear, just lend an ear
To the Three Melodious Mice!"

A fat mole dressed in a jester suit entered. He ran at the singing trio with a pailful of water and launched the contents at them.

Everybeast screamed and covered their eyes. Surely the three pretty singers would be drenched!

But it was only a pailful of flower petals! The audience breathed a sigh of relief, laughing and clapping. Hypericum Haddock Hare bellowed into his big, curly seashell:

"For your amusement! Comical capers, jolly japes, marvelous mirth, and a rib-ticklin' rumpus! From our very own Droll Dumplin's an' Cavortin' Clowns!"

Whooping and tumbling, a band of moles, voles, and dormice, all comically dressed, took the floor.

Exploding cakes? For goodness' sakes!
Do slapsticks really smart?
That silly grin upon his face
brings laughter to your heart!

Bungo and Tubspike roared with merriment. Tears streamed from their eyes. Skipper of otters and Matthias held their sides, chuckling.

The hare announced the next performer. "Father Abbot, good Redwallers all, allow me to present . . . theeeeeee one an' only Mighty Bulbrock Broadstripe!"

A gasp arose from the audience. Bulbrock Broadstripe the badger shed his flowing cape. Twirling his curled mustachio, he bowed, then rearing up, he flexed his powerful muscles and issued a warning to Bungo, Tubspike, and all the little ones watching.

"Never h'attempt to perform the things h'I am h'about to do, h'as you might h'injure your liddle selves!"

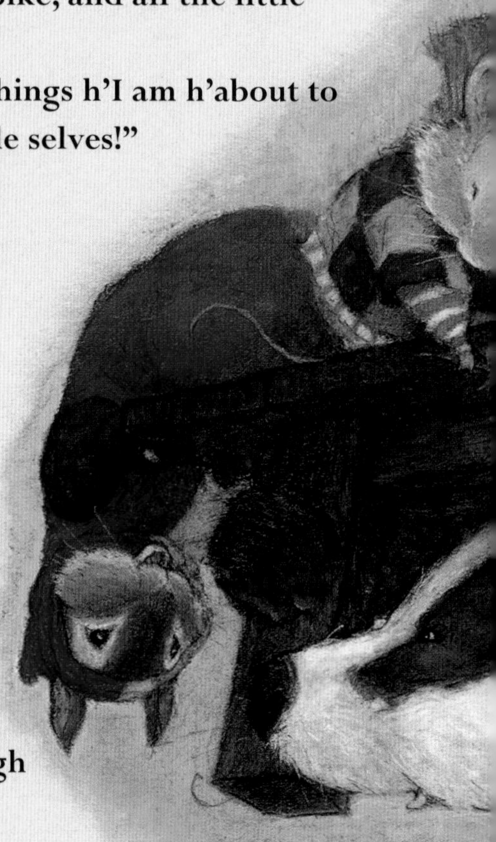

He flung a big stone ball up high
and caught it with both paws;
a solid bar of iron he took
and bent it in his jaws!

Then he took two metal weights,
which no four beasts could shift,
and swung them up above his head,
all in one easy lift!

The hare, six squirrels, and eight mice
upon a table sat. . . .
He carried all twice 'round Great Hall!
Now what d'you think of that?

"Whoa, lukkout, zurrs!" Foremole and Noisy Sam ducked their heads, just in time.

A dozen apples whizzed through the air like magic. It was Oswald and Oriole, the Juggling Otters! 'Round and 'round the apples flew between the juggling duo. Oswald and Oriole did all this while balancing upon two rounded logs. Not only that, but they both spun balls on their tailtips, crying out:

"Hoopla, rosy apples for all!
Hoopla, will we let one fall?
Up they comes, down they goes,
where they lands, nobeast knows!"

Seizing items from the festive tables, they added them to the whirling medley. Sugarplums, pears, and candied chestnuts whizzed with the apples over the diners' heads. Oswald and Oriole skillfully changed the flying fruit into different patterns, chanting as they did:

"Hark, little 'uns, this trick is yours.
Hold out both your open paws,
sit quite still now, close your eyes,
and here's a sweet surprise!"

Bungo, Tubspike, and all the Abbeybabes squeaked with delight. A candied chestnut landed, plop! into each of their small paws. Oswald and Oriole bowed and beamed at the well-deserved applause they received.

Such skill!

Alley oop! Head over tail,
high above the Abbey floor,
see amid the rafter beams
the Flying Firgrove Squirrels soar!

Catch your partner by the paw,
loop the loop and somersault.
Whirling free up in midair,
the Flying Firgrove Squirrels vault!

Fearless, those skilled acrobats,
each one born with nerves of steel,
hurtling, twirling gracefully,
the Flying Firgrove Squirrels wheel!

Magical Mugwort amazes all.
In a cloud of smoke he'll appear
to vanish a spoon from Bungo's paw
and produce it out of his ear!

Abracadabra! Alakazam!
He gives his wand a shake,
bees fly out of the Abbot's sleeve,
and daisies sprout from a cake!

What a mysterious hedgehog!
"How does he do it?" they cry,
whilst from a tiny nutshell
ribbons and streamers fly.

Does Mugwort do it with mirrors?
Is it all a trick, a joke?
How what why, who knows? Not I.
Whoof! He's gone in a cloud of smoke!

Redwallers were beside themselves with merriment and admiration of the Troupe. Applauding heartily, they cheered and pounded the tables.

Good Father Abbot called out to the performers, "What a marvelous show! Come now, friends, please sit with us and share our feast!"

At a nod from Hadduck Hare, the entire Troupe took a bow and hurried to places set for them at the table. And what a table for hungry entertainers it was!

Whilst the feasting and chatting continued, Constance the Badgermum cast an eye over the Abbeybabes. Most of them were rubbing their eyes and yawning.

"Come on, my Dibbuns, time you were snug in your beds."

The babes snuffled and grumbled. But Bungo complained aloud, "Gurr, et b'aint furr. Whoi shudd uz likkle 'uns go t'bed, an' ee big 'uns stay oop? Oi b'aint agoin', no marm!"

Mighty Bulbrock Badger swept Bungo up in one huge paw. "Hearken to me, liddle master mole. H'if you wants to grow h'up big'n'strong like me, you'll go right h'off to bed! Besides, tonight h'is Autumn's final day, so you must go."

Mighty Bulbrock winked at the dozy Dibbuns. "Come on, h'I'll tell you h'all a story once you're h'all h'in bed."

Bungo cheered up a bit. "Ho gudd, ee bedtoime story, oi do loikes them, zurr!"

Up the winding Abbey stairs
little paws go plodding.
In the flick'ring lantern light
tiny heads are nodding.
Side by side, wearily,
snail-like Dibbuns creep.
Redwall's spiral staircase
leads to the land of sleep.

With Constance, Cornflower, and several others to help, it was not long before the Abbeybabes were tucked up snug in their little dormitory beds, some already asleep.

But not Bungo. "Tell uz ee story, zurr!"

So Mighty Bulbrock told the tale, a story known to all creatures, as old as time itself.

Old Autumn's final day is done
when midnight bells toll Winter's birth.
That is the time, so legend says,
Snow Badger comes to earth!
Awakened in his realms of sky
to visit earth below,
unseen by any living eye;
thus, it was ever so.

Lord of cold Winter season,
he makes all stars shine bright,
ruler of the icy winds,
whose breath can freeze the night!

But if anybeast should see him
before his work's complete,
oh, woe to us, calamity!
Snow Badger would retreat.

He'd leave no Wintertide at all,
no blanket white and deep,
to let poor Mother Nature rest
her earth in peaceful sleep.
And if there were no Winter?
Why, then there'd be no Spring.
No crops to mow, no flowers to grow,
no little birds to sing!
Our lands would turn to desert,
how sorry we'd all be.
So eyes shut tight! Sleep sound tonight!
Let Snow Badger roam free!

Mighty Bulbrock's voice was so deep and comforting that all the Abbeybabes were soon fast asleep, dreaming their own small dreams.

On tip paw, the elders stole out and went downstairs, chuckling to one another: "Snow Badger, eh, that's a good story to make them sleep!" "Aye, I can remember my old grandma telling it to me." "Me, too. Hahaha, and I believed it, every word!"

Mighty Bulbrock toyed with something on a string about his neck. He looked at them in surprise. "You don't believe the story of the Snow Badger anymore?"

"Believe it? Haha, not us, it's only an old bedtime story to make babes go to sleep!"

But Mighty Bulbrock Badger did not laugh.

'Twas late that night, all banqueting was done.
Redwallers and their guests to bed had gone.
Outside the North Wind howled in dirgelike moans,
scouring at the Abbey's ancient stones.
Within, each creature slumbered, safe and warm,
heedless to the songs of wind or storm.
Fires grew low as solid pine logs burned;
their wood to glowing embers slowly turned.
This was the time he had been waiting for:
Old Lord of Wintertide arrived once more.

High, high above, midst the vast acres of dense nightcloud, Snow Badger strode. Thrice taller than the greatest oak he stood. Glittering silverwhite was his coat. Above the two pearl-grey stripes which marked his massive face, a crown of pure ice wreathed his hoary head.

The Lord of Wintertide's eyes were of the palest blue. He gazed down at the earth, many leagues below, laid bare by the dying breath of Autumn's wind. Behind him, as far as any eye could see, legion upon legion of his white Snow Hares stood waiting.

Snow Badger's voice rolled across the dark vaults of night to them.

"Go you now at my command,
as you have done each year.
Let allbeasts know, throughout the land,
their Lord of Wintertide is here!
Sheet the sleeping earth in white,
leave nought uncovered in your wake.
Soft and silent, toil all night
'til dawn's first light doth break."

The Snow Hares went then. Like all the stars from the Milky Way falling from the heavens, countless, myriad hordes of them, quietly drifting, down, down, for the sighing winds to strew them over the slumbering ground.

Twirling, swirling, sifting, drifting,
driven as the wild winds bid,
see the armies turn to snow,
sacrificed, 'til all is hid.
Hedgerow, field, and woodland
disappear from sight,
smooth becomes the landscape
'neath a cloak of white.
Sticking to old Abbey walls,
piling deep 'round door and sill,
seeking out each niche or cranny,
searching for a ditch to fill.

Numbing, muffling, mute, and silent,
Winter closes tight its vise,
sheening pond and lake up tight,
locking fish beneath the ice.
Now the brook has ceased to chuckle,
look, the stream is choked and slow.
Icicles form stalactites,
long from eaves they grow.
Down black chimneys, on red embers,
snowflakes sizzle, hiss, and die.
Wintertide is now upon us,
so say all, and so say I!

And so while the snow continued piling up outside, the good creatures of Redwall Abbey slept snug in their beds.

Father Abbot dreamt of next Summer's long, warm days. Skipper of otters dreamt of broad, sunlit streams. Foremole dreamt of digging new tunnels next Spring. The Traveling Thistledown Troupe dreamt of taking the high road to more spectacular performances. Abbeybabes and Dibbuns dreamt of last Summer's golden days, picking strawberries in the orchard patch. Everybeast had calm dreams of peace and leisure.

Except Baby Bungo.

In his roguish dreams Bungo stole pies and puddings from the kitchen windowsills where they stood cooling. He dreamt of growing up to be a big mole without once taking a bath. He dreamt of snow, of stealing out early and pelting everybeast with snowballs until they cried out for mercy!

Bungo gave small villainous chuckles as he dreamt.

Then came the dawn.

Snow Badger drifted regally down from the clouds and looked around at the Winter he had created. The wind died down as the giant Lord of Wintertide strode the land, leaving in his wake not a single pawprint.

Everything was perfect. The entire countryside was pretty as a picture, spotless white. Then he saw Redwall Abbey and suddenly remembered.

Windows!

Only Snow Badger could frost up windowpanes with his icy breath. He hurried to perform the task before the Redwallers awakened, an inner voice calling urgently to him: "Hurry, it is already dawn of Winter's first day!"

Whoosh! His icy breath blew forth,
frosting the gatehouse pane,
patterns of flowers and twinkling stars,
repeating again and again.

Towering high o'er the Abbey,
Snow Badger bent to Great Hall;
colorful stained-glass windows,
with a whoosh, he froze them all!

On to Redwall's kitchens then,
an icy blast he cast.
No cook could peer through windows
patterned and frosted that fast.

Whilst frosting the dormitory windows,
he was facing the final bay,
when the window opened, and Bungo appeared
to bid the Snow Badger good day!

"Gudd day to ee, zurr, be you ee Snow Badger?"

The giant Lord of Wintertide was so astonished that he could only stand glaring at the cheeky little molebabe.

Bungo leaned out and shook one of his whiskers heartily. "Oi be's Bungo an' oi berleeves in ee. You'm vurry noice!"

Snow Badger smiled then, his great face lighting up with delight. Gently he took Bungo onto his outstretched paw.

The little molebabe hung on to one of the mighty claws, looking down at the Abbey, far below. "Hurr! B'aint 'arf 'igh oop yurr, zurr. Be you agoin' to take oi oop to ee clouds with ee?"

Snow Badger laughed then. He laughed so hard that his mighty breath chased the grey cloud banks away. Winter sun beamed down on the land, giving the snow a soft, creamy color and making it sparkle gaily. He shook his big, striped head.

"Oh no, you young rascal, no,
back to your home you must go,
but remember me each Wintertide,
for 'twas I who brought you snow!"

Bungo felt himself lowered to the ground so fast that it made his tiny head spin. He landed softly in a deep snowdrift beside the Abbey door.

Snow Badger shook his head fondly, chuckled, and rose into the clear blue Winter's morn, light as thistledown and free as the breeze, now that his work was done.

The Abbey door swings open wide
as happy young ones tumble out,
all muffled up and bright-eyed,
just hear them squeak and shout:

"Where's a hill to roll down?
Where's a pond to skate?
Snowballing, tobogganing,
oh, isn't Winter great!"

Good Father Abbot and Hypericum Hadduck Hare, with the elders, followed the youngsters out into the snow.

Skipper of otters began clearing a path with his spade. “Well, well, I see old Snow Badger visited us last night.”

Bungo’s head popped up out of the snowdrift beside the door. “Hurr hurr, ee surrtingly did, zurr. Oi see’d ’im!”

Mighty Bulbrock Badger nodded and played with the string about his neck. But the rest of the grown-up Redwallers smiled. Father Abbot patted Bungo fondly.

"Well, golly gosh and goodness me,
Snow Badger showed himself to you.
He must have been a sight to see,
just think a moment, was it true?

"Mayhap last night you closed your eyes
and saw Snow Badger in a dream,
but in the morn, 'tis no surprise
that dreams may not be what they seem!

"Last night you may have eaten too much;
as you grow up, no doubt you'll find
that cheese and pudding, pie and stuff
return to haunt one's mind!"

Bungo waved his little paws, protesting aloud. "Et wurrn't no dream. Oi see'd ee gurt Snow Badger. Ee wurr noice t'me. Lukkit, thurr ee goes!"

All eyes followed the molebabe's paw, which was pointing skyward at an object high in the clear blue sky.

Constance patted Bungo's head fondly. "You little rogue, that's only a cloud!"

"No, it h'aint, marm, that's the Snow Badger. Oi'd know 'im anywheres!"

Mighty Bulbrock Broadstripe, the Traveling Thistledown Troupe's strong badger, stepped forward. He picked Bungo up. "When h'I was h'only this liddle tyke's size, h'I saw the Snow Badger, too. H'I knows Bungo saw 'im. Look!"

He pointed to the string about Bungo's neck. It had a small bag hanging from it. Bungo was as surprised as anybeast. "Burr, wot be's this, zurr?"

Bulbrock showed him the one he was wearing. It was the same. "H'I got this from Snow Badger, h'early one first Winter's morn. H'I was h'awake, and saw 'im afore h'anybeast. He gave me this h'as a gift. H'open the bag, young 'un."

Bungo fumbled with the string (which was really a single hair from the giant badger). He loosed the neck of the bag and shook it. Out fell a scrap of parchment—with something wrapped up in it!

A clear crystal drop, for goodness' sake,
cold and true as a mountain lake,
like a teardrop shed by a star from the sky,
twinkling, glittering, dazzling the eye.

Such pictures shone in that wondrous thing,
deep sunset at sea, a rainbow in Spring,
dawn's light over hills, a wild waterfall,
one just had to look to imagine it all.

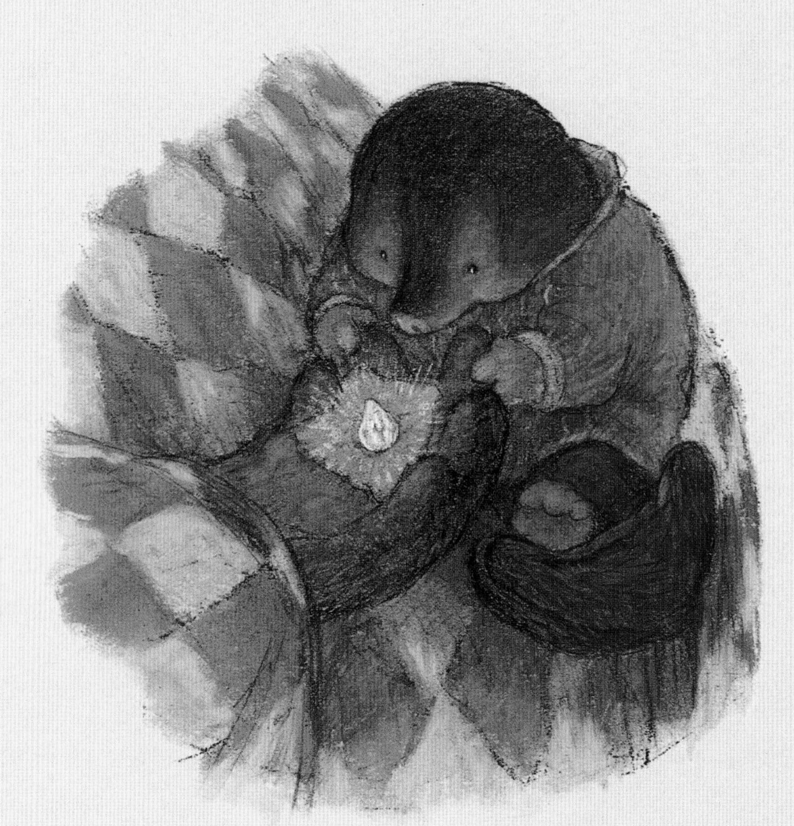

"Now read what the parchment says," Bulbrock advised.

Bungo turned the scrap of parchment this way and that. He scratched his snub nose in puzzlement.

Good Father Abbot smiled kindly at the molebabe's efforts. "Here, little one, you don't start at Abbey School until next Summer. Let me read it for you."

It was a very mysterious little poem that the Abbot of Redwall Abbey read aloud.

Die written a last cry,
There find dearer of,
Off thus poor threat,
It formed her love.

The Redwallers were at a loss to explain the odd rhyme.

"Well, what d'you make of that?"

"What's it supposed to mean?"

"I can't make head nor tail of it."

"Do you know what it means, Father Abbot?"

The Abbot shook his wise old head. "Alas, no, but I'll wager our friend Bulbrock does."

The strong badger chuckled. "H'I knows what h'it means, Father h'Abbot. 'Twas written h'on my scrap o' parchment, too, though h'it took me long h'ages afore h'I managed to solve the riddle of yon poem."

Bulbrock winked at Bungo. "But today h'is Winter's first day, 'tis a time for sport an' play. H'if you haven't guessed the h'answer by h'evenin', h'I'll tell you at supper. What d'you say, liddle mate?"

Bungo nodded his agreement. "You'm be full o' gudd ideas, zurr. Oi loikes t'play!"

And play they did, everybeast young and old.

Constance the Badgermum helped Matthias and Cornflower to build a fine snowmouse. Bungo and Tubspike flung snowballs at them!

Foremole and a crowd of Dibbuns tobogganed down a slope. Bungo and Tubspike giggled, and flung snowballs at them, too!

Skipper and his otters skated figures of eight on the frozen pond. Bungo and Tubspike chuckled, and flung snowballs at them, too!

Good Father Abbot and the Flying Firgrove Squirrels busied themselves, making a snowhouse. Bungo and Tubspike laughed, and flung snowballs at them, too!

Hypericum Hare and some of his Troupe started rolling together a great snowball. Bungo and Tubspike roared with glee. And flung snowballs at them, too!

Blowing plumes of white steam, bright-eyed and rosy-cheeked, everybeast enjoyed themselves thoroughly. But none more than those two little rascals, Bungo and Tubspike. They snowballed anything that moved!

So everybeast left off what they were doing and began snowballing back at the roguish pair. Soon the air was filled with soft white snowballs.

A snowball landed on Foremole's head,
Constance took two on her snout,
one big and fat knocked Bungo flat,
as snowballs whizzed about.
Back and forth they battled,
whop! thud! splotch! and whack!
Look, there goes a laughing hedgehog,
six snowballs stuck to his back!
Nobeast was spared from the riotous fun,
even good old Father Abbot
was forced to flee, smiling gleefully,
pelted from whiskers to habit!

Such fun! They played in the snow until evening, when the skies were glowing scarlet and the sun sank into the far horizons.

Friar Hugo appeared at the Abbey door and rang his bell, squeaking aloud to the revelers:

> "Supper's ready, the bread is hot,
> pies and pastries, fresh mint tea,
> woodland stew, straight from the pot,
> so wipe those paws and follow me!"

Bungo knocked the Friar's tall hat off with a well-aimed snowball as he went inside.

Such fun!

Weary, warm, and well fed, the Redwallers and their guests sat around a roaring log fire in Cavern Hole. A few snowflakes fell down the chimney, hissing as they melted in the heat.

Mighty Bulbrock nodded to Bungo. "H'our Snow Badger's h'at his work again tonight, matey."

Hypericum Hadduck Hare, who was still munching, waved a long ear at Bulbrock. "Now will y'kindly tell us what that little poem means?"

Good Father Abbot interrupted. He drew forth a parchment from his sleeve.

"It's a rhyme within a rhyme. The letters of each line can be changed to explain it. Look."

Wide-eyed with wonder, they looked. Father Abbot was surely the wisest mouse that ever lived.

Die written a last cry, . .	A Wintertide crystal,
There find dearer of, . . .	Dear friend, for thee.
Off thus poor threat, . . .	As proof of the truth
It formed her love.	Hold it ever for me.

Constance the Badgermum shook her head in wonderment. "So that was the solution. The letters of each line have to be switched about to form a new verse. Father Abbot, how wonderful of you to solve the riddle!"

Bungo yawned and rubbed his eyes. "Oi solved et moiself this mornin', but oi wurrn't goin' to tell ee 'til tomorrer, marm!"

Mighty Bulbrock took Bungo upon his lap. "Yore a champion snowball thrower, liddle Bungo, but yore a dreadful fibber!"

Everybeast at Redwall laughed and laughed, all the way up to their beds.

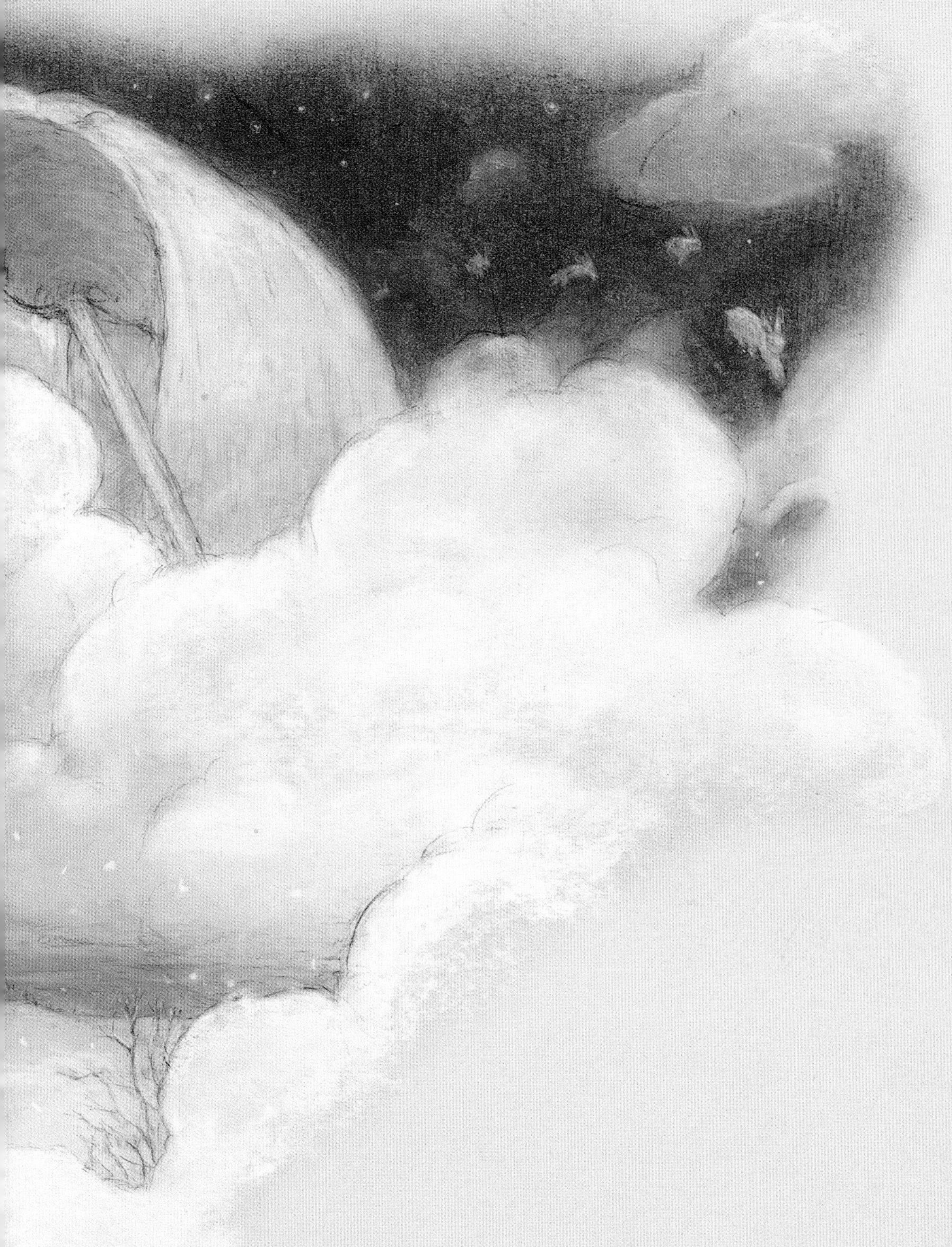

Far up in the cold night skies, Snow Badger watched his hares drifting down to earth and turning to snowflakes. He heard the happy laughter drifting up through the Abbey windows. No doubt his little molefriend Bungo had caused it.

Lying down on a vast, soft cloud, the Lord of Wintertide closed his eyes in slumber. He liked visiting Redwall Abbey to bring Winter joys to its creatures.

Did you enjoy your visit to Redwall, my little friend? I hope you did. Please come back someday, be it Summer, Spring, Autumn, or Winter.

You are always very welcome here!